The Dangers of Smoking in Bed is a work of fiction. Names, characters, places, and incidents either are the product of the author's imagination or are used fictitiously. Any resemblance to actual persons, living or dead, events, or locales is entirely coincidental.

Library of Congress Cataloging-in-Publication Data
Names: Enriquez, Mariana, author. | McDowell, Megan, translator.
Title: The dangers of smoking in bed : stories / Mariana Enriquez ; translated by Megan McDowell.
Description: First edition. | London ; New York : Hogarth, [2020] | Originally published in Spain as Los peligros de fumar en la cama by Editorial Anagrama in Barcelona, Spain, 2017.
Identifiers: LCCN 2020003911 (print) | LCCN 2020003912 (ebook) | ISBN 9780593134078 (hardcover) | ISBN 9780593134085 (ebook)
Subjects: LCSH: Enriquez, Mariana--Translations into English.
Classification: LCC PQ7798.15.N75 A2 2020 (print) | LCC PQ7798.15.N75 (ebook) | DDC 863/.64--dc23
LC record available at https://lccn.loc.gov/2020003911
LC ebook record available at https://lccn.loc.gov/2020003912

Printed in Canada

randomhousebooks.com

10 9 8 7 6 5 4 3 2 1

First Edition

Book design by Debbie Glasserman

The Dangers
of Smoking in Bed

The Dangers
of Smoking
in Bed

Stories

Mariana Enriquez

Translated by Megan McDowell

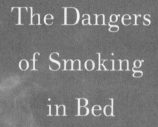

HOGARTH
London / New York

Translation copyright © 2021 by Penguin Random House LLC

All rights reserved.
Published in the United States by Hogarth, an imprint of the Random House Publishing Group, a division of Penguin Random House LLC, New York.

HOGARTH is a trademark of the Random House Group Limited and the H colophon is a trademark of Penguin Random House LLC.

Originally published in Spain as *Los peligros de fumar en la cama* by Editorial Anagrama in Barcelona, Spain. Copyright © 2017 by Mariana Enriquez.

Grateful acknowledgment is made to W. W. Norton & Company, Inc. for permission to reprint an excerpt from "A Sucker's Evening" from *Songs of Love and Horror: Collected Lyrics of Will Oldham* by Will Oldham. Copyright © 2018 by Will Oldham. Reprinted by permission of W. W. Norton & Company, Inc.

Library of Congress Cataloging-in-Publication Data
Names: Enriquez, Mariana, author. | McDowell, Megan, translator.
Title: The dangers of smoking in bed : stories / Mariana Enriquez ; translated by Megan McDowell.
Description: First edition. | London ; New York : Hogarth, [2020] | Originally published in Spain as Los peligros de fumar en la cama by Editorial Anagrama in Barcelona, Spain, 2017.
Identifiers: LCCN 2020003911 (print) | LCCN 2020003912 (ebook) | ISBN 9780593134078 (hardcover) | ISBN 9780593134085 (ebook)
Subjects: LCSH: Enriquez, Mariana--Translations into English.
Classification: LCC PQ7798.15.N75 A2 2020 (print) | LCC PQ7798.15.N75 (ebook) | DDC 863/.64--dc23
LC record available at https://lccn.loc.gov/2020003911
LC ebook record available at https://lccn.loc.gov/2020003912

Printed in Canada

randomhousebooks.com

10 9 8 7 6 5 4 3 2 1

First Edition

Book design by Debbie Glasserman

For Paul and for Chatwin, our kitten

Stay here while I get a curse
To give him a goat head
Make him watch me take his place
Night has brought him something worse

—WILL OLDHAM, "A SUCKER'S EVENING"

Contents

The Dangers
of Smoking in Bed

Angelita Unearthed

My grandma didn't like the rain, and before the first drops fell, when the sky grew dark, she would go out to the backyard with bottles and bury them halfway, with the whole neck underground; she believed those bottles would keep the rain away. I followed her around asking, "Grandma why don't you like the rain why don't you like it?" No reply— Grandma dodged my questions, shovel in hand, wrinkling her nose to sniff the humidity in the air. If it did eventually rain, whether it was a drizzle or a thunderstorm, she shut the doors and windows and turned up the volume on the TV to drown out the sound of wind and the raindrops on the zinc roof of the house. And if the downpour coincided with her favorite show, *Combat!*, there wasn't a soul who could get a word out of her, because she was hopelessly in love with Vic Morrow.

I just loved the rain, because it softened the dry earth and let me indulge in my obsession with digging. And boy, did I dig! I used the same shovel as Grandma, a very small one, like a child's beach toy only made of metal and wood instead of plastic. The plot at the far end of the yard held little pieces of green glass with edges so worn they no longer cut you, and smooth stones that seemed like round pebbles or small beach rocks—what were those things doing out behind my house? Someone must have buried them there. Once, I found an oval-shaped stone the size and color of a cockroach without legs or antennae. On one side it was smooth, and on the other side some notches formed the clear features of a smiling face. I showed it to my dad, thrilled because I thought I'd found myself an ancient artifact, but he told me it was just a coincidence that the marks formed a face. My dad never got excited about anything. I also found some black dice with nearly invisible white dots. I found shards of apple-green and turquoise frosted glass, and Grandma remembered they'd once been part of an old door. I also used to play with worms, cutting them up into tiny pieces. It wasn't that I enjoyed watching the mutilated bodies writhe around before going on their way. I thought that if I really cut up the worm, sliced it like an onion, ring by ring, it wouldn't be able to regenerate. I never did like creepy-crawlies.

I found the bones after a rainstorm that turned the back patch of earth into a mud puddle. I put them into a bucket I used for carrying my treasures to the spigot on the patio, where I washed them. I showed them to Dad. He said they were chicken bones, or maybe even beef bones, or else they were from some dead pet someone must have buried a long time ago. Dogs or cats. He circled back around to the chicken story because before, when he was little, my grandma used to have a coop back there.

It seemed like a plausible explanation until Grandma found out about the little bones. She started to pull out her hair and shout, "Angelita! Angelita!" But the racket didn't last long under Dad's glare: he put up with Grandma's "superstitions" (as he called them) only as long as she didn't go overboard. She knew that disapproving look of his, and she forced herself to calm down. She asked me for the bones and I gave them to her. Then she sent me off to bed. That made me a little mad, because I couldn't figure out what I'd done to deserve that punishment.

But later that same night, she called me in and told me everything. It was sibling number ten or eleven, Grandma wasn't too sure—back then they didn't pay so much attention to kids. The baby, a girl, had died a few months after she was born, suffering fever and diarrhea. Since she was an *angelita*—an innocent baby, a little angel, dead before she could sin—they'd wrapped her in a pink cloth and propped her up on a cushion atop a flower-bedecked table. They made little cardboard wings for her so she could fly more quickly up to heaven, but they didn't fill her mouth with red flower petals because her mother, my great-grandmother, couldn't stand it, she thought it looked like blood. The dancing and singing lasted all night, and they even had to kick out a drunk uncle and revive my great-grandmother, who fainted from the heat and the crying. There was an indigenous mourner who sang Trisagion hymns, and all she charged was a few empanadas.

"Grandma, did all this happen here?"

"No, it was in Salavina, in Santiago. Goodness, was it hot there!"

"But these aren't the baby's bones, if she died there."

"Yes, they are. I brought them with us when we moved. I didn't want to just leave her, because she cried every night, poor thing. And if she cried when we were close by, just imagine how she'd cry if she was all alone, abandoned! So I brought her. She was nothing but little bones by then, and I put her in a bag and buried her out back. Not even your grandpa knew. Or your great-grandma, no one. It's just that I was the only one who heard her cry. Well, your great-grandpa heard too, but he played dumb."

"And does the baby cry here?"

"Only when it rains."

Later I asked my dad if the story of the little angel baby was true, and he said my grandma was very old and could talk some nonsense. He didn't seem all that convinced, though, or maybe the conversation made him uncomfortable. Then Grandma died, the house was sold, I went to live alone with no husband or children, my dad moved to an apartment in Balvanera, and I forgot all about the angel baby.

Until she appeared in my apartment ten years later, crying beside my bed one stormy night.

The angel baby doesn't look like a ghost. She doesn't float and she isn't pale and she doesn't wear a white dress. She's half rotted away, and she doesn't talk. The first time she appeared, I thought it was a nightmare and I tried to wake up.

When I couldn't do it and I started to realize she was real, I screamed and cried and pulled the sheets over my head, my eyes squeezed tight and my hands over my ears so I couldn't hear her—at that point I didn't know she was mute. But when I came out from under there some hours later, the angel baby was still there, the remnants of an old blanket draped over her shoulders like a poncho. She was pointing her finger toward the outside, toward the window and the street, and that's how I realized it was daytime. It's weird to see a dead person during the day. I asked her what she wanted, but all she did was keep on pointing, like we were in a horror movie.

I got up and ran to the kitchen to get the gloves I used for washing dishes. The angel baby followed me. And that was only the first sign of her demanding personality. I didn't hesitate. I put the gloves on and grabbed her little neck and squeezed. It's not exactly practical to try and strangle a dead person, but a girl can't be desperate and reasonable at the same time. I didn't even make her cough; I just got some bits of decomposing flesh stuck to my gloved fingers, and her trachea was left in full view.

So far, I had no idea that this was Angelita, my grandmother's sister. I kept squeezing my eyes shut to see if she would disappear or I would wake up. When that didn't work, I walked around behind her and I saw, hanging from the yellowed remains of what I now know was her pink shroud, two rudimentary little cardboard wings that had chicken feathers glued to them. Those should have disintegrated after all these years, I thought, and then I laughed a little hysterically and told myself that I had a dead baby in my kitchen, that it was my great-aunt and she could walk, even though judging by her size she hadn't lived more than three months. I had to definitively stop thinking in terms of what was possible and what wasn't.

I asked if she was my great-aunt Angelita—since there hadn't been time to register her with a legal name (those were different times), they always called her by that generic name. That's how I learned that even though she didn't speak, she could reply by nodding. So my grandmother had been telling the truth, I thought: the bones I'd dug up when I was a kid weren't from any chicken coop, they were the little bones of Grandma's sister.

It was a mystery what Angelita wanted, because she didn't do anything but nod or shake her head. But she sure did want something, and badly, because not only did she constantly keep pointing, she wouldn't leave me alone. She followed me all over the house: she waited for me behind the curtain when I showered, she sat on the bidet anytime I was on the toilet, she stood beside the fridge while I washed dishes, and she sat beside my chair when I worked at the computer.

I went about my life more or less normally for the first week. I thought maybe the whole thing was a hallucination brought on by stress, and that she would eventually disappear. I asked for some days off work; I took sleeping pills. But the angel baby was still there, waiting beside the bed for me to wake up. Some friends came to visit me. At first I didn't want to answer their messages or let them in, but eventually I agreed to see them, to keep them from worrying even more. I claimed mental exhaustion, and they understood; "You've been working like a slave," they told me. None of them saw the angel baby. The first time my friend Marina came to visit me, I stuck the angel in the closet. But to my horror and disgust, she escaped and sat right down on the arm of the sofa with that ugly, rotting, gray-green face of hers. Marina never knew.

Not long after that, I took the angel baby out into the street. Nothing. Except for that one man who glanced at her in passing and then turned around and looked again and his face crumpled—his blood pressure must have dropped; or the lady who started running straight away and almost got hit by the 45 bus in Calle Chacabuco. Some people must see her, I figured, but it sure wasn't many. To save them from the shock, when we went out together—or rather, when she followed me out and I had no choice but to let her—I used a kind of backpack to carry her (it's gross to see her walk— she's so little, it's unnatural). I also bought her a bandage to use as a mask, the kind burn victims use to cover their scars. Now when people see her, they're disgusted, but they also feel compassion and pity. They see a very sick or injured baby, but not a dead baby.

If only Dad could see me now, I thought. He had always complained that he was going to die without grandchildren (and he did die without grandchildren, I disappointed him in that and in many other ways). I bought her toys to play with, dolls and plastic dice and pacifiers she could chew on, but she didn't seem to like anything very much, she just kept on with that damned finger pointing south—that's what I realized, it was always southward—morning, noon, and night. I talked to her and asked her questions, but she just wasn't a very good communicator.

Until one morning she turned up with a photo of my childhood home, the house where I had found her little bones in the backyard. She got it from the box where I keep old photos: disgusting, she left all the other pictures stained with her rotten flesh that peeled off, damp and slimy. Now she was pointing at the picture of the house, really insistent. "You want to go there?" I asked her, and she nodded yes. I explained that the house no longer belonged to us, that we'd sold it, and she nodded again.

I loaded her into the backpack with her mask on and we took the 15 bus to Avellaneda. When we're traveling, she doesn't look out the window or around at other people, she doesn't do anything to entertain herself; the outside world matters as much to her as the toys I bought her. I carried her sitting on my lap so she'd be comfortable, though I don't know if it's possible for her to be uncomfortable, or if that concept even means anything to her; I don't know what she feels. All I know is that she isn't evil, and that I was afraid of her at first, but I'm not anymore.

We reached the house that used to be mine at around four in the afternoon. As always in summer, a heavy smell of the Riachuelo River and gasoline hung over Avenida Mitre, mixed with the stench of garbage. We walked across the plaza and past the Itoiz hospital, where my grandmother had died, and finally we went around the Racing stadium. Two blocks past the field we came to my old house. But what to do now that I was at the door? Ask the new owners to let me in? With what excuse? I hadn't even thought about that. Clearly, carrying a dead baby around everywhere I went had affected my mind.

It was Angelita who took charge of the situation, pointing her finger. We didn't need to go inside. We could peer into the backyard over the dividing wall; that was all she wanted— to see the backyard. The two of us looked in as I held her up—the wall was pretty low, it must have been poorly made. There, where the earthen square of our backyard used to be, was a blue plastic swimming pool set into the ground. Apparently, they'd dug up all the earth to make the hole, and who knows where they'd thrown the angel baby's bones, shaken up, lost. I felt bad for her, poor little thing, and I told her I was really sorry, but I couldn't fix this for her. I even told her I regretted not having dug up her bones again when the house was sold, so I could rebury them in some quiet place, or close to the family if that's what she wanted. I mean, how hard would it have been to put them in a box or a flowerpot, and bring them home with me! I'd treated her badly and I apologized. Angelita nodded yes. I understood that she forgave me. I asked her if now she was at peace and if she would leave, if she was going to leave me alone. She shook her head no. Okay, I replied, and since her answer didn't sit well with me, I started walking fast toward the 15 bus stop. I made her run after me on her bare little feet that, rotten as they were, left her little white bones in view.

Our Lady of the Quarry

Silvia lived alone in a rented apartment of her own, with a five-foot-tall pot plant on the balcony and a giant bedroom with a mattress on the floor. She had her own office at the Ministry of Education and a salary; she dyed her long hair jet black and wore Hindu shirts with sleeves wide at the wrists and silver thread that shimmered in the sun. She had the provincial last name of Olavarría and a cousin who had disappeared mysteriously while traveling around Mexico. She was our "grown-up" friend, the one who took care of us when we went out and who let us use her place to smoke weed and meet up with boys. But we wanted her ruined, helpless, destroyed. Because Silvia always knew more: If one of us discovered Frida Kahlo, oh, Silvia had already visited

Frida's house with her cousin in Mexico, before he disappeared. If we tried a new drug, she had already overdosed on the same substance. If we discovered a band we liked, she had already *gotten over* being a fan of the same group. We hated that she had long, heavy, straight hair, colored with a dye we couldn't find in any normal beauty salon. What brand was it? She probably would have told us, but we would never ask. We hated that she always had money, enough for another beer, another twenty-five grams, another pizza. How was it possible? She said that in addition to her salary she had access to her father's account; he was rich, she never saw him, and he hadn't recognized paternity, but he did deposit money for her in the bank. It was a lie, surely. As much a lie as when she said her sister was a model: we'd seen the girl when she came to visit Silvia and she wasn't worth three shits, a runty little skank with a big ass and wild curls plastered with gel that couldn't have gotten any more greasy. I'm talking low-class—that girl couldn't dream of walking a runway.

But above all we wanted her brought down because Diego liked her. We'd met Diego in Bariloche on our senior class trip. He was thin and had bushy eyebrows, and he always wore a different Rolling Stones shirt (one with the tongue, another with the cover of *Tattoo You*, another with Jagger clutching a microphone whose cord morphed into a snake). Diego played us songs on the acoustic guitar after the horseback ride when it got dark near Cerro Catedral, and later on in the hotel he showed us the precise measurements of vodka and orange juice to make a good screwdriver. He was nice to us, but he only wanted to kiss us, he wouldn't sleep with us, maybe because he was older (he'd repeated a grade, he was eighteen), or maybe he just didn't like us that way. Then, once we were back in Buenos Aires, we called to invite him to a party. He paid attention to us for a while, until Silvia started chatting him up. And from then on he kept treating us well, it's true, but Silvia totally took over and kept him enthralled (or overwhelmed: opinions were divided), telling stories about Mexico and peyote and sugar skulls. She was older too, she'd been out of high school for two years. Diego hadn't traveled much, but he wanted to go backpacking in the north that year. Silvia had already made that trip (of course!), and she gave him advice, telling him to call her for recommendations on cheap hotels and families who would rent out rooms, and he bought every word, in spite of the fact that Silvia didn't have a single photo, not one, as proof of that trip or any other (she was quite the traveler).

Silvia was the one who came up with the idea of the quarry pools that summer, and we had to give it to her, it was a really good idea. Silvia hated public pools and country club pools, even the pools at estates or weekend houses: she said the water wasn't fresh, she always felt like it was stagnant. Since the nearest river was polluted, she didn't have anywhere to swim. We were all like, "Who does Silvia think she is, she acts like she was born on a beach in the south of France." But Diego listened to her explanation of why she wanted "fresh" water and he was totally in agreement. They talked a little more about oceans and waterfalls and streams, and then Silvia mentioned the quarry pools. Someone at her work had told her you could find a ton of them off the southern highway, and that people hardly ever went swimming there because they were scared, supposedly the pools were dangerous. And that's where she suggested we all go the next weekend, and we agreed right away because we knew Diego would say yes, and we didn't want the two of them going alone. Maybe if he saw how ugly her body was—she had some really tubby legs, which she claimed were because she'd played hockey when she was little, but half of us had played hockey too, and none of us had those big ham hocks. Plus she had a flat ass and broad hips, which was why jeans never fit her well. If he saw those defects (plus the black hairs she never really got rid of—maybe she couldn't pull them out down to the root, she was really dark), maybe Diego would stop liking Silvia and finally pay attention to us.

She asked around a little and decided we had to go to the Virgin's Pool, which was the best, the cleanest. It was also the biggest, deepest, and most dangerous of all. It was really far, almost at the end of the 307 route, after the bus merged onto the highway. The Virgin's Pool was special, people said, because almost no one ever went there. The danger that kept swimmers away wasn't how deep it was: it was the owner. Apparently someone had bought the place, and we accepted that: none of us knew what a quarry pool was good for or if it could be bought, but still, it didn't strike us as odd that the pool would have an owner, and we understood why this owner wouldn't want strangers swimming on his property.

It was said that when there were trespassers, the owner would drive out from behind a hill and start shooting. Sometimes he also set his dogs on them. He had decorated his private quarry pool with a giant altar, a grotto for the Virgin on one side of the main pool. You could reach it by going around the pool along a dirt path to the right, a path that started at an improvised entrance from the road, marked by a narrow iron arch. On the other side was the hill over which the owner's truck could appear at any moment. The water in front of the Virgin was still and black. On the near side, there was a little beach of clayey dirt.

We went every Saturday that January. The heat was torrid and the water was so cold: it was like sinking into a miracle. We even forgot Diego and Silvia a little. They had also forgotten each other, enchanted by the coolness and secrecy. We tried to keep quiet, to not make any racket that could wake the hidden owner. We never saw anyone else, although sometimes other people were at the bus stop on the way back, and they must have assumed we were coming from the quarry because of our wet hair and the smell that stuck to our skin, a scent of rock and salt. Once, the bus driver said something strange to us: that we should watch out for wild dogs on the loose. We shivered, but the next weekend we were as alone as ever, we didn't even hear a distant bark.

And we could see that Diego was starting to take an interest in our golden thighs, our slender ankles, our flat stomachs. He still kept closer to Silvia and he still seemed fascinated, even if by then he'd realized that we were much, much prettier. The problem was that the two of them were very good swimmers, and although they played with us in the water and taught us a few things, sometimes they got bored and swam off with fast, precise strokes. It was impossible to catch up with them. The pool was really huge; we'd stay close to the shore and watch their two heads bobbing on the surface, and we could see their lips moving but had no idea what they were saying. They laughed a lot, that's for sure, and Silvia's laugh was raucous and we had to tell her to keep it down. The two of them looked so happy. We knew that very soon they would remember how much they liked each other, and that the summer coolness near the highway was temporary. We had to put a stop to it. *We* had found Diego, and she couldn't keep everything for herself.

Diego looked better every day. The first time he took off his shirt, we discovered that his shoulders were strong and hunched, and his back was narrow and had a sandy color, just above his pants, that was simply beautiful. He taught us to make a roach clip out of a matchbook, and he watched out for us to make sure we didn't get in the water when we were too crazy—he didn't want us getting high and drowning. He ripped CDs of the bands that according to him we just had to hear, and later he'd quiz us; it was adorable how he got all happy when he could tell we'd really liked one of his favorites. We listened devotedly and looked for messages—was he trying to tell us something? Just in case, we even used a dictionary to translate the songs that were in English; we'd read them to each other over the phone and discuss them. It was very confusing—there were all kinds of conflicting messages.

All speculation was brought to an abrupt halt—as if a cold knife had sliced through our spines—when we found out that Silvia and Diego were dating. When! How! They were older, they didn't have curfews, Silvia had her own apartment, how stupid we were to apply our little-kid limitations to them. We snuck out a lot, sure, but we were controlled by schedules, cellphones, and parents who all knew each other and drove us places—out dancing or to the rec center, friends' houses, home.

The details came soon enough, and they were nothing spectacular. Silvia and Diego had been seeing each other without us for a while; at night, in effect, but sometimes he went to pick her up at the Ministry and they went for a drink, and other times they slept together at her apartment. No doubt they smoked pot from Silvia's plant in bed after sex. We were sixteen, and some of us hadn't had sex yet, it was terrible. We'd sucked cock, yes, we were quite good at that, but fucking, only some of us had done that. Oh, we just hated it. We wanted Diego for ourselves. Not as our boyfriend, we just wanted him to screw us, to teach us sex the same way he taught us about rock and roll, making drinks, and the butterfly stroke.

Of all of us, Natalia was the most obsessed. She was still a virgin. She said she was saving herself for someone who was worth it, and Diego was worth it. And once she got something into her head, she'd hardly ever back down. Once, she'd taken twenty of her mom's pills when her parents had forbidden her from going dancing for a week—her grades were a disaster. In the end they let her go dancing, but they also sent her to a psychologist. Natalia skipped the sessions and spent the money on stuff for herself. With Diego, she wanted something special. She didn't want to throw herself at him. She wanted him to want her, to like her, she wanted to drive him crazy. But at parties, when she went to talk to him, Diego flashed her a smile and went on with his conversation with whichever of us he was talking to. He didn't answer her calls, and if he did, the conversations were always languid and he was always the one to end them. At the quarry pool he didn't stare at her body, her long, strong legs and firm ass, or else he looked at her like he would a pretty boring plant—a ficus, for example. Now, *that* Natalia couldn't believe. She didn't know how to swim, but she got wet near the shore and then came out of the water with her yellow swimsuit stuck to her tan body so tight you could see her nipples, hard from the cold water. And Natalia knew that any other boy who saw her would kill himself jacking off, but not Diego, no—he preferred that flat-assed skank! We all agreed it was incomprehensible.

One afternoon, when we were on our way to PE class, Natalia told us she'd put menstrual blood in Diego's coffee. She'd done it at Silvia's house—where else! It was just the three of them, and at one point Diego and Silvia went to the kitchen for a few minutes to get coffee and cookies; the coffee was already served on the table. Real quick, Natalia poured in the blood she'd managed to collect—very little—in a tiny bottle from a perfume sample. She'd wrung out the blood from cotton gauze, which was disgusting; she normally used pads or tampons, the cotton was just so she could get the blood. She diluted it a little in water, but she said it should work all the same. She'd gotten the technique from a parapsychology book, which claimed that while the method was not very hygienic, it was an infallible way to snag your beloved.

It didn't work. A week after Diego drank Natalia's blood, Silvia herself told us they were dating, it was official. The next time we saw them, they couldn't keep their hands off each other. That weekend when we went to the quarry pool they were holding hands, and we just couldn't understand it. We couldn't understand it. The red bikini with hearts on one of us; the super-flat stomach with a belly button piercing on another; the exquisite haircut that fell just so over the face, legs without a single hair, underarms like marble. And he preferred her? Why? Because he screwed her? But we wanted to screw too, that was *all* we wanted! How could he not realize, when we sat on his lap and pressed our asses into him, or tried to brush our hands against his dick like on accident? Or when we laughed near his mouth, showing our tongues. Why didn't we just throw ourselves at him, once and for all? Because it was true for all of us, it wasn't just an obsession of Natalia's: we wanted Diego to choose us. We wanted to be with him still wet from the cold quarry water, to fuck him one after the other as he lay on the little beach, to wait for the owner's gunshots and run to the highway half-naked under a rain of bullets.

But no. There we were in all our glory, and he was over kissing on old, flat-ass Silvia. The sun was burning and flat-ass Silvia's nose was peeling, she used the crappiest sunscreen, she was a disaster. We, though, were impeccable. At one point, Diego seemed to realize. He looked at us differently, as if comprehending he was with an ugly skank. And he said, "Why don't we swim over to the Virgin?" Natalia went pale, because she didn't know how to swim. The rest of us did, but we didn't dare cross the quarry, so long and deep and if we started to drown there was no one to save us, we were in the middle of nowhere. Diego read our thoughts: "How about Sil and I swim over, you guys walk along the edge and we'll meet there. I want to see the altar up close. Are you up for it?"

We said yes, sure, though we were concerned because if he was calling her "Sil" then maybe our impression that he was looking at us differently was wrong, and we were just so desperate for it to be true that we were going kind of crazy. We started to walk. Getting around the quarry wasn't easy: it seemed much smaller when you were sitting on the little beach. It was huge. It must have been three blocks long. Diego and Silvia went faster than us, and we saw their dark heads appear at intervals, shining golden under the sun, so luminous, and their arms plowing slippery through the water. At one point they had to stop, and we watched from the shore—under the sun, dust plastered to our bodies with sweat, some of us with headaches from the heat and the harsh light in our eyes, walking as if uphill—we saw them stop and talk, and Silvia laughed, throwing her head back and treading water with her arms to stay afloat. It was too far to swim in one go, they weren't professionals. But Natalia got the feeling that they didn't stop just because they were tired, she thought they were plotting something. "That bitch has something up her sleeve," she said, and she kept walking toward the Virgin we could barely see inside the grotto.

Diego and Silvia reached the Virgin's grotto just as we were turning right to walk the final fifty yards. They must have seen the way we were panting, our armpits stinking like onion and our hair stuck to our temples. They looked at us closely, laughed the same way they had when they'd stopped swimming, and then they jumped right back into the water and started swimming as fast as they could back to the little beach. Just like that. We heard their mocking laughter along with the splash. "Bye, girls!" Silvia shouted triumphantly as she set off swimming, and we were frozen there in spite of the heat—weird, we were frozen and more boiling hot than ever, our ears burning in shame as we cast about desperately for a comeback and watched them glide away, laughing at the dummies who didn't know how to swim. Humiliated, fifty yards away from the Virgin that now no one felt like looking at, that none of us had ever really wanted to see. We looked at Natalia. She was so filled with rage that the tears wouldn't fall from her eyes. We told her we should go back. She said no, she wanted to see the Virgin. We were tired and ashamed, and we sat down to smoke, saying we would wait for her.

She took a long time, about fifteen minutes. Strange—was she praying? We didn't ask her, we knew very well how she was when she got mad. Once, she'd bitten one of us in an attack of rage, for real, she left a giant bite mark on the arm that had stayed there for almost a week. Finally she came back, asked us for a drag—she didn't like to smoke whole cigarettes—and started to walk. We followed her. We could see Silvia and Diego on the beach, drying each other off. We couldn't hear them well, but they were laughing, and suddenly a shout from Silvia, "Don't get mad, girls, it was just a joke."

Natalia whirled around to face us. She was covered in dust. There was even dust in her eyes. She stared at us, studying us. Then she smiled and said:

"It's not a Virgin."

"What?"

"It has a white sheet to hide it, to cover it, but it's not a Virgin. It's a red woman made of plaster, and she's naked. She has black nipples."

We were scared. We asked her who it was, then. Natalia

said she didn't know, it must be a Brazilian thing. She also said she'd asked it for a favor. And that the red was really well painted, and it shone, like acrylic. That the statue had very pretty hair, long and black, darker and silkier than Silvia's. And when she approached it, the false virginal white fell on its own, she didn't touch it, like the statue wanted Natalia to see it. Then she'd asked it for something.

We didn't reply. Sometimes she did crazy things like that, like the menstrual blood in the coffee. Then she'd get over it.

We reached the beach in a very bad mood, and we ignored all of Silvia and Diego's attempts to make us laugh. We saw them start to feel guilty. They said they were sorry, asked our forgiveness. They admitted it had been a bad joke, mean, designed to embarrass us, mean and condescending. They opened the little cooler we always brought to the quarry and took out a cold beer, and just as Diego flipped off the cap with his keychain-opener, we heard the first growl. It was so loud, clear, and strong that it seemed to come from very close by. But Silvia stood up and pointed to the hill where the owner supposedly could appear. It was a black dog, though the first thing Diego said was, "It's a horse." No sooner did he finish the word, the dog barked, and the bark filled the afternoon and we could have sworn it made the surface of the water in the quarry pool tremble a little. It was big as a pony, completely black, and it was clearly about to come down the hill. But it wasn't the only one. The first growl had come from behind us, at the end of the beach. There, very close to us, three slobbering pony-dogs were walking. You could see their ribs as their sides rose and fell—they were skinny. These were not the owner's dogs, we thought, they were the

dogs the bus driver had told us about, savage and dangerous. Diego made a "shhh" sound to soothe them, and Silvia
said, "We can't show them we're scared." And then Natalia,
furious, finally crying now, screamed at them: "You arrogant
assholes, you're a flat-ass skank, and you're a shithead, and
those are my dogs!"

There was one ten feet away from Silvia. Diego didn't
even hear Natalia: he stood in front of his girlfriend to pro-
tect her, but then another dog appeared behind him, and
then two smaller ones that came running and barking down
the hill where the owner never did turn up, and suddenly
they started howling, from hunger or hatred, we didn't know.
What we did know, what we realized because it was so obvi-
ous, was that the dogs didn't even look at us. None of us.
They ignored us, it was like we didn't exist, like it was only
Silvia and Diego there beside the quarry pool. Natalia put on
a shirt and a skirt, whispered to us to get dressed too, and
then she took us by the hands. She walked to the iron arch
over the entranceway that led to the highway, and only then
did she start to run to the 307 stop; we followed her. If we
thought about getting help, we didn't say anything. If we
thought about going back, we didn't mention that either.
When we got to the highway and heard Silvia's and Diego's
screams, we secretly prayed that no car would stop and hear
them too; sometimes, since we were so young and pretty, people stopped and offered to take us to the city for free. The 307
came and we got on calmly so as not to raise suspicions. The
driver asked us how we were and we told him, fine, great, it's
all good, it's all good.

The Cart

Juancho was drunk that day. He was getting belligerent as he walked up and down the sidewalk, although by that point no one in the neighborhood felt threatened, or even unsettled, by his drunken antics. Halfway down the block, Horacio was washing his car like he did every Sunday, in shorts and flip-flops, his prominent belly taut, his chest hair white, the radio tuned to the game. On the corner, the Spaniards from the variety store were drinking *mate* with the kettle on the ground between the two folding recliners they'd brought outside because the sun was nice. Across the way, Coca's boys were drinking beer in the doorway, and a group of girls, freshly bathed and overly made-up, were chatting as they stood in the doorway of Valeria's garage. Earlier, my dad had tried to say hi and start a conversation with the neighbors, but he came back inside as always, downcast, a little annoyed, because he was a good guy but he didn't know small talk—he said the same things every Sunday afternoon.

My mom was spying out the window. She got bored with the Sunday TV, but she didn't feel like going out. She peered between the half-open blinds, and would occasionally ask us to bring her a cup of tea, or a cookie, or an aspirin. My brother and I usually spent Sundays at home; sometimes, at night, we'd take a spin downtown if Dad would lend us the car.

Mom saw him first. He was coming from the direction of Tuyutí's corner, walking in the middle of the street and pushing a loaded-down supermarket cart. He was even drunker than Juancho, but somehow he managed to push that pile of garbage in the cart—all bottles, cardboard, and phone books. He stopped in front of Horacio's car, swaying. It was hot that day, but the man was wearing an old, greenish pullover. He must have been around sixty years old. He left the cart at the curb, went over to the car, and, right on the side where my mother had the best view, he pulled down his pants.

She called to us to come see. We came to the window and all three of us peered through the blinds with her: my brother, my dad, and me. The man, who wasn't wearing underwear under his filthy dress pants, shat on the sidewalk: soft shit, almost diarrhea, and a lot of it. The smell reached us, and it stank as much of alcohol as it did of shit.

"Poor man," said my mom.

"A person can come to such misery," said my dad.

Horacio was stupefied, but you could tell he was about to

get mad, because his neck was turning red. But before he could react, Juancho ran across the street and pushed the man, who hadn't even had time to stand up, or pull up his pants. The old man fell into his own shit, which spattered onto his sweater and his right hand. He only murmured an "Oh."

"Black-ass bum!" Juancho shouted at him. "You vagrant son of a bitch, how dare you come here and shit on our neighborhood, you uppity cocksucking scumbag!"

He kicked the man on the ground. Juancho was wearing flip-flops, and his feet also got spattered with shit.

"Get up, you bastard, you get up and hose down Horacio's sidewalk—you can't fuck around here—and then get back to whatever slum you crawled out of, you son of a motherfucking bitch."

And he went on kicking the man, in the chest, in the back. The man couldn't get up; he seemed not to understand what was happening. Suddenly he started to cry.

"It's not worth all that," said my dad.

"How can he humiliate the poor man like that?" said my mom, and she stood up and headed for the door. We followed her. When Mom got to the sidewalk, Juancho had gotten the man up, whimpering and apologizing, and was trying to shove into his hands the hose Horacio had been using to wash the car, so he could wash away his own shit. The whole block stank. No one dared approach. Horacio said, "Juancho, leave it," but in a low voice.

My mom intervened. Everyone respected her, especially Juancho, because she would give him a few coins for wine when he asked her. The others treated her with deference because though Mom was a physical therapist, everyone thought she was a doctor, and that's what they all called her.

"Leave him alone. Let him go, it's fine. We'll clean up. He's drunk, he doesn't know what he's doing, there's no cause to hit him."

The old man looked at Mom, and she told him, "Sir, apologize and be on your way." He murmured something, dropped the hose, and, still with his pants down, tried to push the cart away.

"The doctor saved your life, you asshole, but the cart stays here. You pay for your filth, dirty-ass trespasser, you don't fuck around in this neighborhood."

Mom tried to dissuade Juancho, but he was drunk, and furious, and he was shouting like a vigilante, and there was nothing white left in his eyes, only black and red, the same colors as the shorts he was wearing. He stood in front of the cart and he wouldn't let the man push it. I was afraid another fight would break out—another pounding from Juancho, really—but the man seemed to give up. He zipped up his pants—they didn't have a button—and walked off, in the middle of the street again, toward Catamarca; everyone watched him go, the Spaniards murmuring *how awful,* Coca's boys cackling, some of the girls in Valeria's garage laughing nervously, others with their heads down, as though ashamed. Horacio cursed under his breath. Juancho took a bottle from the cart and threw it at the man, but it missed him by a long shot and shattered against the concrete. The man, startled by the noise, turned around and shouted something unintelligible. We didn't know if he was speaking another language (but which?), or if he was simply too drunk to articulate. But before running off in a zigzag, fleeing from Juancho, who was chasing him and shouting, he looked straight at my mom, fully lucid, and nodded twice. He said something else, rolling his eyes, taking in the whole block and more. Then he disappeared around the corner. Juancho was too wasted to follow. He just went on yelling for a long time.

Everyone went inside. The neighbors would go on talking about the episode all afternoon, and all week long. Horacio used the hose, all grumbling and "Fucking bums, fucking bums."

"What can you expect from this neighborhood," said Mom, and she closed the blinds.

Someone, probably Juancho himself, moved the cart to Tuyutí's corner and left it parked in front of the house Doña Rita had left empty when she died the year before. After a few days, no one payed it any attention. At first they did, because they expected the *villero*—what else could he be but a slum-dweller?—to come back for it. But he never turned up, and no one knew what to do with his things. So there they stayed, and one day they got wet in the rain, and the damp cardboard disintegrated and gave off a smell. Something else stank amid all the junk, probably rotting food, but disgust kept people from cleaning. It was enough to give the cart a wide berth, walk real close to the houses and not look at it. There were always gross smells in the neighborhood, coming from the greenish muck that flowed along the gutters, or from the Riachuelo when a certain breeze blew, especially at dusk.

It all started around fifteen days after the cart arrived. Maybe it started before that, but there had to be an accumulation of misfortune for the neighborhood to feel like something strange was going on. Horacio was the first. He had a rotisserie downtown, and it did well. One night, when he was balancing the register, some thieves came in and took it all. These things happen. But that same night, after filing the report—useless, as in most robberies, among other reasons because the thugs wore masks—when Horacio went to the ATM to take out money, he found out he didn't have a single peso in his account. He called the bank, made a fuss, kicked in doors, tried to throat punch an employee, and he took things to the branch manager, and then to the regional manager. But there was nothing for it: the money wasn't there, someone had taken it out, and Horacio, from one day to the next, was ruined. He sold his car. He got less for it than he expected.

Coca's two boys lost the jobs they had in the auto repair shop on the avenue. Without warning; the owner didn't even give them explanations. They yelled and cursed at him, and he kicked them out. Then, to top it off, Coca's pension didn't come through. Her sons spent a week looking for work, and after that they set to squandering their savings on beer. Coca got into bed saying she wanted to die. No one would give them credit anywhere. They didn't even have bus fare.

The Spaniards had to close the variety store. Because it wasn't just Coca's boys, or Horacio; every one of the neighbors, all of a sudden, in a matter of days, lost everything. The merchandise at the kiosk disappeared mysteriously. The taxi driver's car was stolen. Mari's husband and only support, a bricklayer, fell off a scaffold and died. The girls had to leave their private schools because their parents couldn't afford them; the dentist had no more clients, neither did the dressmaker, and a short-circuit blew out all the butcher's freezers. After two months no one in the neighborhood had a phone anymore—they couldn't afford it. After three months, they had to tap the electricity wires because they couldn't pay their bills. Coca's boys went out to pickpocket and one of them, the most inept, got caught by the police. Then one night the other one didn't come home; maybe he'd been killed. The taxi driver ventured on foot to the other side of the avenue. There, he said, everything was fine as could be. Up to three months after it all started, businesses on the other side of the avenue gave credit. But eventually, they stopped.

Horacio put his house up for sale.

Everyone locked their houses with old chains, because there was no money for alarms or more effective locks; things started to go missing from houses, TVs and radios and stereos and computers, and you'd see some neighbors lugging appliances between two or three of them, hoisted in their arms or loaded into shopping carts. They took it all to pawnshops and used-appliance stores across the avenue. But other neighbors organized, and when the thieves tried to knock down their doors, they brandished knives, or guns if they had them. Cholo, the vegetable vender around the corner, cracked the taxi driver's skull with the iron he used for grilling. At first, a group of women organized to ration out the food that was left in the freezers, but when they discovered that some people lied and kept supplies for themselves, the goodwill went all to hell.

Coca ate her cat, and then she killed herself. Someone had to go to the Social Services office on the avenue for them to take away the body and bury it for free. One of the employees there wanted to find out more, and the neighbors told him, and then the TV cameras came to record the localized bad luck that was sinking three blocks of the neighborhood into misery. They especially wanted to know why the neighbors farther away, the ones who lived four blocks over, for example, didn't show solidarity.

Social workers came and handed out food, but that only led to more wars breaking out. At five months, not even the police would come in, and the people who still went to watch TV on the display sets in the appliance stores on the avenue said that the news talked of nothing else. But soon the neighbors were totally isolated, because when the people on the avenue recognized them, they were shooed away.

The neighbors were isolated, I say, because we did have TV, and electricity, and gas, and a phone. We said we didn't, and we lived as battened down as the rest; if we met someone on the street, we lied: we ate the dog, we ate the plants, Diego—my brother—got credit at a store twenty blocks from here. My mom managed things so she could go out to work, jumping from roof to roof (it wasn't so hard in a neighborhood where all the houses were low). My dad could take out his pension from an ATM, and we paid our services online, because we still had internet. No one sacked our house; respect for the doctor, maybe, or very good acting on our part.

One day, Juancho was sitting on the sidewalk drinking wine straight from the bottle that he'd stolen from a distant supermarket. He was the one who started to yell and curse:

"It's the fucking cart, the *villero*'s cart." He yelled for hours, spent hours walking the street, banging on doors and windows: "It's the cart, it's the old man's fault, we have to go find him, let's go, you pieces of shit, he put some kind of macumba curse on us." Juancho's hunger showed more than the others' because he'd never had anything before, he lived off the coins he collected every day, ringing doorbells (people always gave him something, out of fear or compassion, who knows). That same night he set the cart on fire, and the neighbors watched the flames out their windows. And Juancho was right about something. Everyone had thought it was the cart. Something in it. Something contagious it had brought from the slum.

That same night, my dad gathered us into the dining room for a family meeting. He told us that we had to leave. That people were going to realize we were immune. That Mari, the next-door neighbor, already suspected something, because it was pretty hard to hide the smell of food, even though when we cooked we took care to seal the openings around the door so the smoke and the smells didn't waft out. Our luck was going to run out; everything went bad. Mom agreed. She told us she'd been spotted jumping over the back roof. She couldn't be sure, but she'd felt eyes on her. Diego too. He said that one day, when he raised the blinds, he'd seen some neighbors running away, but others had stayed and stared at him, defiant; bad ones, crazy by now. Almost no one saw us, we stayed locked in the house, but to keep up the charade we would have to go out soon. And we weren't skinny or gaunt. We were scared, but fear doesn't look the same as desperation.

We listened to Dad's plan, which didn't seem very reasonable. Mom told us hers, and it was a little better, but nothing out of this world. We all agreed on Diego's: my brother's way of thinking was always more simple and matter-of-fact.

We went to bed, but none of us could sleep. After tossing and turning, I knocked on my brother's door. I found him sitting on the floor. He was really pale from lack of sun—we all were. I asked him if he thought Juancho was right. He nodded.

"Mom saved us. Did you see how the man looked at her, before he left? She saved us."

"So far," I said.

"So far," he said.

That night, we smelled burnt meat. Mom was in the kitchen and we went in to reprimand her—was she crazy, putting a steak on the grill at that hour? People were going to catch on. But Mom was trembling beside the counter.

"That's not regular meat," she said.

We opened the blinds a crack and looked up. We saw the smoke coming from the terrace across from us. And it was black, and it didn't smell like any other smoke we knew.

"Damn old ghetto son of a bitch," said Mom, and she started to cry.

The Well

I am terrified by this dark thing
That sleeps in me;
All day I feel its soft, feathery turnings, its malignity.

SYLVIA PLATH, "ELM"

Josefina remembered the trip—the heat, the crowded Renault 12—like it was just a few days ago, and not back when she was six, just after Christmas, under the stifling January sun. Her father drove, barely speaking; her mother was in the passenger seat and Josefina was in back, stuck between her sister and her grandma Rita, who was peeling mandarins and flooding the car with the smell of overheated fruit. They were going to Corrientes on vacation, to visit her aunt and uncle on her mother's side, but that was only part of the larger reason for the trip, which Josefina couldn't even guess at. No one spoke much, she remembered. Her grandmother and her mother both wore dark glasses, and they only opened their mouths to warn of a truck passing too close to the car, or to beg her father to slow down; they were tense and alert and waiting for an accident.

They were afraid. They were always afraid. In summer, when Josefina and Mariela wanted to swim in the above-ground pool, Grandma Rita filled it with five inches of water, and then sat in a chair in the shade of the patio's lemon tree to keep watch over every splash, so she'd be sure to get there in time if her granddaughters started to drown. Josefina remembered how her mother used to cry and call in doctors and ambulances at dawn if she or her sister had a fever of just a couple degrees. Or how she made them miss school for a harmless cold. She never let them sleep over at their friends' houses, and she hardly ever let them play on the sidewalk; when she did, they could see her keeping watch over them from the window, hidden behind the curtains. Sometimes Mariela cried at night, saying that something was moving under her bed, and she could never sleep with the light off. Josefina was the only one of the family's women who was never afraid; she was like her father. Until that trip to Corrientes.

She couldn't remember how many days they had spent at her aunt and uncle's house, nor if they had gone to the waterfront or to window-shop on the pedestrian walkways. But she remembered the visit to Doña Irene's house perfectly. The sky had been cloudy that day but the heat was heavy, as always in Corrientes before a storm. Her father hadn't gone with them; Doña Irene's house was near her aunt and uncle's, and the four of them had walked there with her aunt Clarita. They didn't call Irene a witch; mostly they just called her The Woman. Her house had a beautiful front yard, a little overfull of plants, and almost right in the center there was a white-painted well. When Josefina saw it, she let go of her grandmother's hand and ran, ignoring the howls of panic, to get a closer look and peer in over the edge. They couldn't stop her until she saw the bottom of the well and the stagnant water in its depths.

Her mother gave her a slap that could well have made Josefina cry, except that she was used to those nervous wallops that ended in sobs and hugs and "My baby, my baby, if anything ever happened to you." Like what? Josefina had thought. She'd never considered jumping into the well. No one was going to push her. She just wanted to see if the water would reflect her face the way wells always did in fairy tales—her face like a blond-haired moon in the black water.

Josefina had fun that afternoon at The Woman's house. Her mother, grandmother, and sister, sitting on stools, had let Josefina nose around among the offerings and knickknacks piled up in front of an altar; Aunt Clarita waited discreetly outside in the yard, smoking. The Woman talked, or prayed, but Josefina didn't remember anything strange—no chanting, no clouds of smoke, no placing of hands on her family. The Woman just whispered to them low enough that Josefina couldn't hear what she was saying, but she didn't care. On the altar she found baby booties, fresh and dried bouquets of flowers, photographs in color and black-and-white, crosses adorned with red cords, a lot of rosaries—plastic, wood, silver-plated metal. There was also the ugly figure of the saint her grandmother prayed to, San La Muerte, Saint Death—a skeleton with its scythe. The figure was repeated in different sizes and materials, sometimes in rough approximations, others carved in detail, with deep black eye sockets and a broad grin.

After a while Josefina got bored and The Woman told her, "Little one, why don't you rest in the armchair, go on now." She did, and she fell asleep immediately, sitting up. When she woke it was nighttime, and Aunt Clarita had gotten tired of waiting for them. They had to walk back on their own. Josefina remembered how, before they left, she'd tried to go back and look into the well, but she couldn't bring herself to do it. It was dark and the white paint shone like the bones of San La Muerte; it was the first time she felt fear. They returned to Buenos Aires a few days later. That first night back in their house, Josefina hadn't been able to sleep when Mariela turned off the light.

Mariela slept soundly in the little bed across from her, and now the night-light was on Josefina's bedside table; she didn't feel tired until the glowing hands of the Hello Kitty clock showed three or four in the morning. Mariela would be hugging a doll, and Josefina would watch its plastic eyes shine humanly in the half dark. Or she'd hear a rooster crow in the middle of the night and remember—but who had told her?—that at that hour of the night a rooster's crow was a sign that someone was going to die. And that had to mean her, so she took her own pulse—she'd learned how by watching her mother, who always checked the girls' heartbeats when they had a fever. If her pulse was too fast, she'd get so scared she wouldn't even dare call her parents to come and save her. If it was slow, she kept her hand against her chest to

be sure her heart didn't stop. Sometimes she fell asleep count-
ing, eyes on the second hand. One night, she discovered that
the blot of plaster on the ceiling just over her bed—a repair
after a leak—was shaped like a head with horns: the face of
the devil. That time she'd told Mariela, but her sister, laughing, said that stains were like clouds, you could see all kinds
of shapes if you looked at them too long. And Mariela didn't
see any devil; to her it looked like a bird on two legs. One
night Josefina heard the neighing of a horse or donkey and
her hands started to sweat at the thought that it had to be the
Mule Spirit, the ghost of a dead woman who'd been turned
into a mule and couldn't rest, and who went out to gallop at
night. That one she'd told her father; he'd kissed her head
and told her those stories were rubbish, and that afternoon
she'd heard him yelling at her mother: "Tell her to stop feed-
ing the girl all that bullshit! I don't want your mother filling
up her head with those superstitions, the ignorant old bag!"
Her grandmother denied telling her any stories, and she
wasn't lying. Josefina had no clue where she'd gotten those
ideas, she just felt like she knew, the same way she knew she
couldn't put her hand to a hot stove without burning herself,
or that in the fall she needed to wear a jacket over her shirt
because it got cool in the evenings.

Years later, sitting across from one of her many psycholo-
gists, she had tried to explain and rationalize her fears one by
one: what Mariela said about the plaster could be true, and
maybe she *had* heard her grandmother tell those stories, they
were part of the Corrientes mythology, and maybe one of the
neighbors had a chicken coop, maybe the mule belonged to
the junk sellers who lived around the corner. But she didn't

believe any of those explanations. Her mother would go to the sessions too, and explain how she and her own mother were "anxious" and "phobic" and they certainly could have passed on those fears to Josefina; but they were recovering, and Mariela no longer suffered from night terrors, and so "Jose's issue" was surely just a matter of time.

But time dragged on for years, and Josefina hated her father because one day he took off and left her alone with those women who, after years of hiding away inside, now planned vacations and weekend outings, while Josefina felt faint when she reached the front door; she hated that she'd had to leave school, and that her mother had to take her at the end of the year to sit for exams; she hated that the only kids who visited her house were Mariela's friends; she hated how they talked about "Jose's issue" in quiet voices, and above all she hated spending days in her room reading stories that at night turned into nightmares. She'd read the story of Anahí and the ceibo flower, and in her dreams a woman had appeared wrapped in flames; she'd read about the potoo bird, and now before she fell asleep she would hear its call, which was really the voice of a dead girl crying near her window. She couldn't go to La Boca because it seemed to her that the river's black surface hid submerged bodies that would surely try to rise up as soon as she got near its edge. She never slept with a leg uncovered, because she just knew she would feel a cold hand touching it. Josefina's mother left her with Grandma Rita when she had to go out; if she was half an hour late Josefina would start to vomit, because the delay could mean only that her mother had died in a car crash. She ran past the portrait of the dead grandfather she'd never met—she could feel his black eyes following her—and she never went near the room that held her mother's old piano, because she *knew* that when no one else was playing it, the devil took a turn.

From the sofa, her hair so greasy it always looked wet, Josefina watched the world she was missing go by. She hadn't even attended her sister's fifteenth birthday party, and she knew Mariela was grateful. She went from one psychiatrist to another for years, and certain pills had allowed her to go back to school, but only until the third year, when she'd discovered that there were other voices in the school's hallways, beneath the hum of kids planning parties and benders. Then there was the time she'd been in a bathroom stall and seen bare feet walking over the tiles, and a classmate told her it must be the suicidal nun who'd hung herself from the flagpole years before. It was useless for her mother and the principal and the school counselor to tell her that no nun had ever killed herself in the schoolyard; Josefina was already having nightmares about the Sacred Heart of Jesus, Christ's open chest that bled and drenched her face in blood, about Lazarus, pale and rotting as he rose from a tomb among the rocks, and about angels that tried to rape her.

And so she'd stayed home, and went back to taking exams at the end of each year with a doctor's excuse. Meanwhile, Mariela was coming home at dawn in cars that screeched to a halt in front of the house, and she heard the kids' shouts at the end of a night of adventure that Josefina couldn't even begin to imagine. She envied Mariela even when her mother was yelling at her about a phone bill that was impossible to pay; if only Josefina had someone to talk to. Because her group therapy sessions sure didn't work; all those kids with real problems—absent parents or violent childhoods—who talked about drugs and sex and anorexia and heartbreak. But she kept going anyway, always in a taxi there and back—and the taxi driver always had to be the same one, and he had to wait for her at the door because she got dizzy and her pounding heart wouldn't let her breathe if she was ever left alone in the street. She hadn't gotten on a bus since that trip to Corrientes, and the only time she'd been in the subway she had screamed until she lost her voice, and her mother had to get her out at the next stop. That time, her mother had shaken her and dragged her up the stairs, but Josefina didn't care, she just had to get out of that confinement any way possible, away from the noise and that snaking darkness.

The new pills—sky blue, practically experimental, shiny like they'd just come from the lab—went down easy, and in just a little while they managed to make the sidewalk seem less like a minefield. They even let her sleep without dreams she could remember, and when she turned out the bedside lamp one night, she didn't feel the sheets grow cold as a tomb. She was still afraid, but she could go to the newsstand alone without the certainty she would die on the way. Mariela seemed more pleased than Josefina was. She suggested they get coffee together, and Josefina got up the nerve to go—in a taxi there and back, of course. That afternoon she'd been able to talk to her sister like never before, and she surprised herself by making plans to go to the movies (Mariela promised to leave half-